KIRSTEN AND THE NEW GIRL

KIRSTEN · 1854

BY JANET SHAW

ILLUSTRATIONS RENÉE GRAEF

VIGNETTES SUSAN MCALILEY

THE AMERICAN GIRLS COLLECTION®

Published by Pleasant Company Publications
Previously published in *American Girl*® magazine
© Copyright 2000 by Pleasant Company
For information, address: Book Editor, Pleasant Company Publications,
8400 Fairway Place, P.O. Box 620998, Middleton, WI 53562.

Printed in Singapore.
00 01 02 03 04 05 06 07 TWP 10 9 8 7 6 5 4 3 2 1

Edited by Nancy Holyoke and Michelle Jones
Designed by Laura Moberly and Kimberly Strother
Art Directed by Kym Abrams and Kimberly Strother

Library of Congress Cataloging-in-Publication Data

Shaw, Janet Beeler, 1937-
Kirsten and the new girl / by Janet Shaw ;
illustrations, Renée Graef; vignettes, Susan McAliley.
p. cm. — (The American girls collection)
Summary: When a new girl arrives at school, Kirsten is jealous, completely
forgetting how scared and lonely she felt the year before when she was
the new girl in school. Gives instructions for making a friendship pillow
like those made in the 1850s.

ISBN 1-58485-034-5
[1. Jealousy Fiction. 2. Schools Fiction. 3. Friendship Fiction.]
I. Graef, Renée, ill. II. Title. III. Series.
PZ7.S53423 Kg 2000 [Fic]—dc21 99-38621 CIP

The
AMERICAN GIRLS
COLLECTION ™

OTHER AMERICAN GIRLS
SHORT STORIES:

FELICITY'S DANCING SHOES

AGAIN, JOSEFINA!

ADDY'S LITTLE BROTHER

SAMANTHA SAVES THE WEDDING

MOLLY AND THE MOVIE STAR

PICTURE CREDITS
The following individuals and organizations have generously given
permission to reprint illustrations contained in "Looking Back": p. 30—tc;
p. 31—tk; p. 32-33—Starr Ockenga Collection; p. 34—Historic Northhampton,
Northhampton, MA; p. 35, 37— Minnesota Historical Society; p. 38—Historical
Society of North Dakota; p. 39—Abby Aldrich Rockefeller Folk Art Center,
Williamsburg, VA; p. 40—Photography by Jamie Young, Prop Styling by Jean do Pico

TABLE OF CONTENTS

KIRSTEN'S FAMILY

PAPA
*Kirsten's father, who
is sometimes gruff
but always loving.*

MAMA
*Kirsten's mother, who
never loses heart.*

KIRSTEN
*A ten-year-old
who moves with her
family to a new
home on America's
frontier in 1854.*

LARS
*Kirsten's fifteen-year-old
brother, who is
almost a man.*

PETER
*Kirsten's mischievous
brother, who is
seven years old.*

LISBETH
*Kirsten's twelve-year-old
cousin.*

ANNA
*Kirsten's eight-year-old
cousin.*

NORA
*The new girl, who just
emigrated from Norway.*

KIRSTEN AND THE NEW GIRL

"M y fever's gone, and my measles spots have almost faded," Kirsten said. "Can I go back to school today, Mama?"

Mama bent over Kirsten's bed and pressed her palm to Kirsten's forehead. "I believe you are well again," Mama said. "Hurry and eat your breakfast and go to meet your cousins."

But Kirsten didn't need to be told to hurry. She was already pulling on her

stockings and searching for her boots
under her bed. For many days a bad case

 of measles had kept her home
from school. At first she was
too sick to miss her friends
or Miss Winston, her teacher.
But as Kirsten began to feel better, she
became more and more lonely. Now that
Mama had pronounced her well, Kirsten
couldn't wait to be back at school with
everyone else.

She gobbled up her pancakes and
was out the door before her brothers,
Lars and Peter, were ready to leave. But
instead of joining her cousins Anna and
Lisbeth at their cabin nearby, Kirsten
decided to hide beside the path to school.

When they came by, she would jump out and surprise them.

It was August, and the prairie flowers bloomed higher than her head. No sooner had Kirsten crept into the tall grass than she heard her cousins' voices as the girls came around the bend of the path.

"She's so pretty!" Anna said in her piping voice.

"And good at sums," Lisbeth said. "She's really clever, don't you think?"

Grasshoppers jumped onto her arms and shoulders, but Kirsten held herself still as her cousins came closer. She wanted to hear more about the pretty, smart girl they were praising.

"I'm so glad her family came to live here!" Anna said.

"Everyone's glad she came," Lisbeth added. "And Miss Winston likes her because she tries so hard at her work."

They must be talking about me, Kirsten thought.

Happily, she pushed through the thick grass and stepped onto the path. "Here I am!"

Anna jumped and dropped her basket. Lisbeth's mouth popped open in surprise. "But you're sick!" the girls exclaimed at the same time.

Kirsten laughed as they hurried to meet her. "I'm well now! I'm going to school with you today."

Happily, Kirsten pushed through the thick grass and stepped onto the path. "Here I am!"

"We missed you!" Anna said, clasping Kirsten's hand and leaning close. "Oh, your face is still pale and a little spotty! You *look* like you've had measles."

"We couldn't visit you because our mama was afraid we'd get measles, too," Lisbeth explained.

"I understand," Kirsten said. Teasing, she nudged Anna's shoulder with hers as they began walking again. "Anyway, we're together again. And I overheard what you were saying just now."

"We were talking about a new girl," Anna said with a smile.

"But I'm really not new anymore," Kirsten said. "We've lived in Minnesota for a whole year."

"Oh, we weren't talking about *you*," Lisbeth corrected her. "We were talking about a girl who came to school for the first time yesterday. Her family's from Norway, so she doesn't speak English very well, but she's better than lots of us in numbers."

Kirsten stepped ahead quickly so she could keep her back to her cousins. She didn't want them to see how her face flamed with embarrassment when she realized her mistake. They hadn't been praising her at all. They were praising a girl Kirsten had never met.

"The new girl's got the sweetest smile," Anna said, skipping to catch up with Kirsten. "Her name's Nora.

7

Everyone likes her because she smiles all the time. You'll like her, too, won't you, Kirsten?"

Kirsten wanted to agree, but no words would come. She was still too embarrassed—and disappointed—to say a thing. Instead, she nodded.

The nod was enough for Anna. "Good. Let's run so you can meet her before Miss Winston rings the bell." Anna scooted ahead, kicking up dust and startling a flock of pigeons from the bushes.

"Wait, I'm not strong enough to run," Kirsten managed to say. "Remember, I've been sick." She felt sorry for herself but didn't want her cousins to know it. She wished they would pay more attention to her before they rushed to the new girl.

❤

Neither Anna nor Lisbeth seemed to notice that Kirsten hung back. They were hurrying to a girl with a thick blond braid who stood with the others in the clearing by the school-house. The new girl had a round face, creamy skin,  and a dimple in her cheek. She was laughing and blushing at everything the other girls said to her. She *was* awfully pretty, Kirsten thought, and wished she'd stayed home until her measles spots had entirely disappeared.

Kirsten walked even more slowly.
The whole time she'd been sick she'd
imagined the moment when she would
come back to school. She'd imagined
how all her friends would welcome her
and how happy she would feel to see
them. Instead, the new girl was the center
of attention.

When Kirsten joined the others, they
made room for her and smiled. Kirsten
tried to smile back, but her lips felt numb.
Maybe I'm still a little sick, she thought.
Yes, it would have been better if she
hadn't come to school at all.

Anna introduced Kirsten to the new
girl. "Nora, here's our cousin! We told
you about her, remember?"

Kirsten tried to smile back, but her lips felt numb.

Nora glanced quickly at Kirsten, then away. A blush reddened Nora's cheeks. Kirsten thought her blue eyes were almost too bright and glittering.

"Hello, Nora," Kirsten said quietly.

Blinking, Nora looked Kirsten's way again. Nora barely nodded a greeting. *She looks like a young deer cornered by dogs,* Kirsten thought.

Kirsten decided not to wait for the bell to ring. She went alone inside the schoolhouse to take her familiar place on the bench in front of the woodstove.

But all day nothing was as Kirsten remembered. Anna helped Nora, not Kirsten, with reading and writing.

12

Miss Winston hovered over Nora and
encouraged all her attempts to write
English words on her slate. At noontime
the girls gathered around Nora and out-
did one another in admiring her apron,
her dress, and the gold chain with a small
cross that she wore around her neck.
When they ate, they competed to see
who would sit next to Nora. At afternoon
recess, Miss Winston asked Nora to read
the marching exercises as they marched
around the schoolyard to get fresh air
into their lungs. *Everything is Nora, Nora,
Nora,* Kirsten thought. It was as though
Powderkeg School belonged to the new
girl now.

All day Kirsten had a sick, green

feeling in her stomach. The feeling left a bitter taste in her mouth and made her weak and dizzy. When Miss Winston said, "Good work, Nora!" for the tenth time, Kirsten's head ached. When Anna put her arm around Nora's waist as they waited in line for a drink of water, Kirsten felt as though she might burst into tears. She hated this feeling of jealousy. She'd never felt it before, and she wished with all her heart it would go away. Most of all she wished Nora would go back to where she'd come from and everything would be just as it was before.

♥

That evening, Kirsten was washing up the supper dishes when Mama stopped clearing the table to stroke Kirsten's forehead. "I'm worried about you," Mama said. "You hardly ate a bite of the good fish I fried, and usually it's your favorite. Your shoulders are slumped, and you didn't say a word when Lars and Peter were talking about school. Did I send you back before you were well enough?"

Kirsten drew away from Mama's touch. She didn't want to admit her bad feelings about the new girl. "I'm hot and the mosquitoes bother me, that's all," she said.

"But it's been hot all summer, and the mosquitoes always bother us," Mama said. "Something else is very wrong. I'm afraid you're getting sick all over again."

Mama's face looked so worried that Kirsten knew she had to admit it wasn't the measles that troubled her. She wiped her hands on her apron and plopped down on the bench by the table. "There's a new girl at our school," she said very softly.

Mama sat beside her. "Ah! From the family that settled near the Halversons' land. Is she a nice girl?"

"I guess so," Kirsten said reluctantly. "She smiles all the time. Everyone is nice to her, especially Anna and Lisbeth."

Mama nodded. "And they *should* be nice to her! It's very hard to be the new one. You remember that, dear. Just a year ago you were new here. You were worried every day when you went to school. But you had your cousins by your side! If you hadn't had a family here you would have had a much harder time."

Mama's reminder wasn't at all what Kirsten wanted to hear. She'd hoped Mama would agree that Nora didn't deserve such special treatment. "I wasn't so pleased with myself as this new girl," she said. "And no one paid so much attention to me." Maybe now Mama would sympathize.

"I think your nose is out of joint," Mama said firmly.

But instead of giving her a hug, Mama tweaked Kirsten's nose. "I think your nose is out of joint," Mama said firmly. "All of us settlers are new here in America. We have to help each other out. Treat the new girl as you'd like to be treated yourself, Kirsten. Will you promise me that?"

Kirsten fought back her tears. Mama didn't understand! Kirsten couldn't say no to Mama's question, but she couldn't say yes gladly. "I promise," she whispered. But in her heart she wished that Nora would disappear.

❤

Kirsten could hardly make herself

get out of bed the next morning. She
 dressed slowly and came
to the table long after
the others. Mama served
raspberries on the pancakes, but Kirsten
didn't taste their sweetness. The very
last thing she wanted was to go to school,
but she couldn't think of any way not
to go. If she said she had a fever again,
she'd be lying. If she hid in the woods
and didn't go to school, Lars and Peter
would tell on her. All she could do was
hang back far behind the others. She
walked so slowly that she couldn't yet
see the schoolhouse when she heard
the morning bell ring.

Suddenly, Kirsten heard rustling in

the bushes beside the path. She pulled aside a branch so she could see what was making the noise. Kneeling under the bush was Nora, her lunch pail clutched to her chest! *Why is she hiding here?* Kirsten wondered.

Kirsten peered in at her. "Didn't you hear the bell?" she said. She shook her finger at Nora the way Miss Winston did when she wanted a student to mind her. "Come on. We're already late."

Nora pressed farther back into the leaves. "I do not want to go to school!"

"But why don't you want to go?" Kirsten was puzzled. "Everyone is so nice to you!"

"Teacher *told* them to be nice," Nora

blurted. "No one knows what I am *really* like."

"Everyone knows you're pretty and good at numbers," Kirsten said. She knelt under the branches so she could see Nora better. Grass and twigs stuck in Nora's hair, and dirt streaked her clothes and face.

"But they do not know I'm shy!" Nora said. "And they talk so loud, so fast! I cannot *think*." She put her finger to her forehead.

"Then why do you smile as though everything is fine?" Kirsten asked.

"If I do not smile, I will cry," Nora said in a trembling voice. In fact, tears were filling her eyes and spilling down

her cheeks. She rubbed at them with her fists. "I want to go back to my own country."

"But you can't go back, Nora," said Kirsten gently. "You're here to stay."

"Do not say so!" Nora cried. She held out her hand as though begging Kirsten to take back her words.

23

Kirsten clasped Nora's hand in hers. Now she remembered clearly that she had felt exactly as Nora did. How could she have forgotten? In her first days at school here she'd felt scared and trapped and homesick for Sweden. No one had seemed to understand her feelings. But her cousins had helped her in those difficult days. Kirsten knew how friendship could make sadness and confusion easier to bear.

So she leaned close to Nora and spoke both slowly and softly. "It might be hard right now, but every day will be a little easier. It just takes time. Soon you won't feel like a new girl anymore. You'll be one of us. At least, that's how it was for me after we came here."

Nora laced her fingers through Kirsten's. "Did it really happen like that to you?"

"Just like that. But I had a lot of help from others," Kirsten admitted. "Then one day, without exactly knowing how, I began to feel at home. You have to be patient. But you can believe me, Nora. You'll be happy here if you don't lose heart. You won't, will you?"

"Oh, no, I won't lose heart!" Nora shook her head so hard her braid swung.

"Do you feel a little bit better?" Kirsten asked.

Nora nodded. "You won't tell the others that I cried, will you?" she said.

"Of course I won't tell that you cried!" Kirsten said. "You can trust me." She pulled some twigs from Nora's hair and wiped the dirt from her cheeks with her handkerchief. Then Kirsten got to her feet and tugged back the branches so Nora could stand up, too.

"Now we'll have to run so Miss Winston won't be too angry with us," Kirsten said. "Come on!"

As Kirsten ran down the path toward school, she glanced back over her shoulder and smiled to see that Nora was running right behind.

JANET SHAW

At 8   Now

When I was 11, I moved from a little school to one that was much bigger. On the first day, I wore my red sweater, hoping the bright color would make someone notice me. The halls were filled with strangers, and I panicked: Who would be my friend? But some of the friends I made that year are still my dearest friends today.

Janet Shaw is the author of the Kirsten books in The American Girls Collection.

LOOKING
BACK
1854

A PEEK INTO
THE PAST

FRIENDSHIP IN 1854

A handmade paper doll

When Kirsten was growing up, girls often showed their affection for their friends with a letter or an act of thoughtfulness. Sometimes they exchanged *friendship tokens*, or gifts.

Children living on the frontier didn't have spending money of their own, so a friendship token from a pioneer girl like Kirsten would have been handmade. She would have made it from the materials and tools she had at hand—needle and thread, scraps of fabric, bits of yarn and lace—or from wood, plants, or other things found on the farm or in the forest.

Kirsten and Singing Bird exchanged buttons, handkerchiefs, feathers, and beads. Girls also exchanged things like paper dolls, wooden tops, bunches of wild-flowers, and hand-made dolls. When girls exchanged

These handmade dolls are sisters.

gifts, they often wrote, "When this you see, remember me."

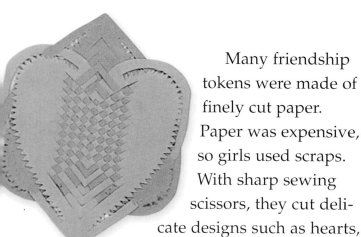

Many friendship tokens were made of finely cut paper. Paper was expensive, so girls used scraps. With sharp sewing scissors, they cut delicate designs such as hearts, wreaths, tulips, doves, and arrows. One cutwork token had two identical hearts woven together to symbolize two friends' hearts locked together forever.

Girls also gave each other locks of their own hair. This was a sign of an especially close friendship, since hair lasted forever. Sometimes a girl gave her friend just a simple lock of hair, or she might twist several strands together to form decorative braids or flowers, or add a small piece of ribbon to make the lock of hair even more special. Strands of hair were also woven, braided, or twisted into jewelry such as necklaces or brooches.

Friendship token with a lock of hair

By the 1850s and 1860s, girls began to exchange photographs of themselves. Photographs had to be taken in a photographer's studio, because cameras were new and expensive and only professionals had them. Girls were posed formally

Three friends posing for a special portrait

with their arms around each other's shoulders or waists, or with their hands clasped. Later, when cameras became less expensive and available to more people, photographs were more casual. Girls were photographed together smiling, laughing, and having fun.

Another way girls and women showed their affection was by making friendship quilts. A friendship quilt was both useful and personal—a girl was warmed by both the quilt itself and the memories it contained. Each square was like a story, made from scraps of familiar clothing and signed by loving relatives and friends. Sometimes they added poems, messages, Bible verses, or sketches.

Friendship quilt

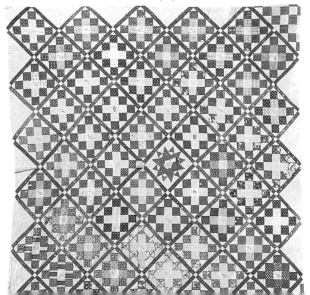

One girl's friendship quilt had this verse:

Accept my friend this little pledge
Your love and friendship to engage
If e'er we should be called to part
Let this be settled in your heart
That when this little piece you see
You ever will remember me.

Friendship quilts became popular as more girls and women moved westward with their families. The quilts were a way to remember the family and friends they had left behind. If each quilter signed her town along with her name, the quilts gave their owners all the information they needed to write their family and friends back home.

When a girl or woman decided to make a quilt for a friend moving far away, she gave quilt *blocks*, or squares, to female family

A signature on a friendship quilt

members and friends to sign. Or she asked family and friends to make and sign their own quilt blocks. After the blocks were finished, everyone gathered for a quilting *bee,* or party. As the girls and women stitched and sewed, they exchanged gossip, news, and recipes. In the evening, the men and children joined them for a meal, music, and dancing.

One type of quilting bee was called

A pioneer quilting bee

a *friendship medley.* A friendship medley
was a two-part party! The first evening
was usually a surprise for the friend
moving away. Everyone gathered together to design their quilt blocks and lay out
the quilt. In the evening, the young men
arrived for supper, dancing, and sometimes kissing games! On the second

evening, everyone sewed the *medley*, or assortment, of blocks together to complete the quilt. When the quilt was finished, each girl could see a bit of herself in the colors and fabrics of the quilt.

These quilters are almost ready for dinner and dancing.

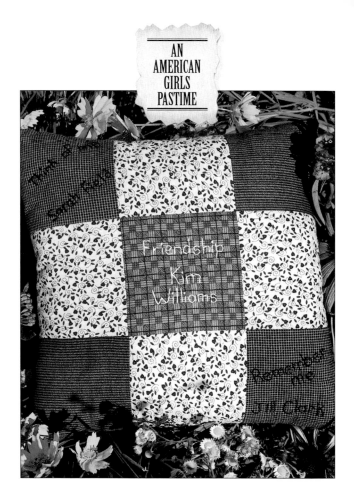

AN
AMERICAN
GIRLS
PASTIME

Friendship

Kim
Williams

Tim & me
Sarah Field

Remember
me
Jill Clark

MAKE A
FRIENDSHIP PILLOW
*Stitch this pillow for a special friend
to remember you by.*

Kirsten was happy to have Nora as her new friend. But she wanted Nora to feel at home at Powderkeg School. To help her feel welcomed, Kirsten might have gathered Anna, Lisbeth, and the other girls together to make Nora a friendship quilt. Show your own friend your affection with a friendship pillow.

YOU WILL NEED:
🖐 *An adult to help you*
9 blocks of cotton fabric in different
patterns, each 5 by 5 inches
Straight pins
Needle
Thread
Scissors
13-inch square of fabric
Cotton for stuffing

1. Give each of your friends a quilt block to sign or write a special message on.

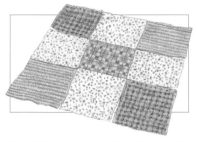

2. When the blocks are finished, lay out the quilt with your friends. Place the nine blocks of fabric in a square, three blocks across and three down.

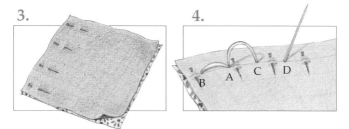

3. In the top strip of the quilt, place the left block on top of the middle block. The "good" sides of the fabric should be face-to-face. Pin the left edges together.

4. Use a backstitch to sew the left edges together, about ¼ inch from the edge. To sew a backstitch, come up at A and go down at B. Come up at C. Then go down at A and come up at D. Keep going. When you've finished, tie a knot close to your last stitch, and cut off the extra thread.

5. Fold the left square out. Now place the right block on top of the middle block with the "good" sides of the fabric face-to-face. Pin the right edges, then sew the blocks together with a backstitch.

6. Repeat steps 3, 4, and 5 with the middle and bottom strips of the quilt.

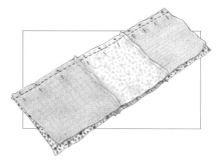

7. Place the top strip facedown on the middle strip. Pin the upper edges together, and sew them together with a backstitch, about ¼ inch from the edge. Fold the top strip up.

8. Place the bottom strip facedown on the middle strip and pin the lower edges together. Then sew them together with a backstitch. Fold the bottom strip down.

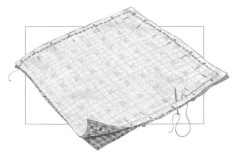

9. Place the 13-inch square of fabric on top of the quilted square, with the "good" sides face-to-face. Pin them together, and sew a backstitch around three sides.

10. Turn the pillow right-side out. Place the stuffing in the pillow. Fold in the edges of the last side and pin them together.

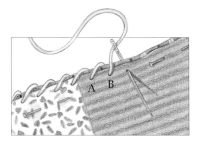

11. Sew up the last side with a whipstitch. Bring the needle up at A, and then pull the thread over the edge to come up at B. When you've finished, remove the pins, tie a knot close to your last stitch, and cut off the extra thread.

THE AMERICAN GIRLS COLLECTION®

To learn more about The American Girls Collection, fill out the postcard below and mail it to American Girl, cr call **1-800-845-0005**. We'll send you a free catalogue full of books, dolls. dresses, and other delights for girls. You can also visit our Web site at **www.americangirl.com**.

I'm an American girl who loves to get mail. Please send me a catalogue of The American Girls Collection:

My name is _____

My address is _____

City _____ State _____ Zip _____

My birth date is ___/___/___ Parent's signature _____
          Month   Day   Year

1961

And send a catalogue to my friend:

My friend's name is _____

Address _____

City _____ State _____ Zip _____

1225